A Fox in Trouble

VISTA®
HIGHER LEARNING

Boston, Massachusetts

SCIENCE

Camila is walking home from school. She hears a sound. She looks. She sees a fox. It's lying on the ground. It's not moving.

"Something is wrong," says Camila. "I need to help the fox." Camila goes to tell her mother.

fox

ground

Camila and her mother call for help. A man comes with a **cage**. He puts it by the fox. The fox doesn't move. He puts food in the cage.

"What do foxes eat?" Camila asks.

"They eat meat," answers the man. "Now we must wait."

cage

3

The fox doesn't move. Then, it slowly lifts its head. It smells the meat. The fox goes into the cage. The man closes it. He takes the fox to an **animal hospital**. Camila and her mother go, too.

"We found this fox," Camila says. "Something is wrong with it."

Dr. Nez is a **veterinarian**. She looks at the fox. She does tests. "This fox is very sick," she says.

"Why is it sick?" Camila asks.

"A mouse ate **poison**," says Dr. Nez. "This fox ate that mouse. The poison made the fox sick."

poison

veterinarian

Camila is worried. She wants the fox to be healthy.

"I gave the fox **medicine**. It's sleeping now," says Dr. Nez. "That fox is lucky you found it. It will stay here. It's still very sick. Come back next week to visit."

Camila and her mother go home. Camila thinks about the fox. She thinks about the poison. "I don't want animals to eat poison," she says. "I don't want animals to get sick. We need to tell people!"

Camila goes to the library. She reads about poisons. She reads about how they affect plants and animals. She learns about the food web. Plants grow in the ground. They're called producers. Animals eat plants and other animals. They're called consumers.

food web

Some animals eat only plants. They're called **herbivores**. Animals like foxes eat mice. They're called **carnivores**. Bigger carnivores like wolves eat foxes. Mice eat poison. The other animals get sick, too. This makes poison dangerous to all the animals.

herbivore

carnivore

"That's not right!" Camila thinks. "People need to know!" She tells her friends about the fox. She tells them about poison. She talks about the food web.

"Oh no! What can we do?" they ask. "We want to help!"

"I know!" says Camila. "We can use the internet. We can tell people."

Camila and her friends make a website. They post information. They write letters, too. They write about poison. They say it hurts animals and plants. They ask people to help.

website

letters

Dear Senator,

Dear Mayor,

Many people see the website. They write comments. They care about animals, too! Camila shows her father. "No more poison?" she asks.

"But I use poison. There are mice in the shed," says her father. "I use **pesticides**, too. They kill weeds in the grass. They kill insects, too."

12 COMMENTS

AnimalFan102,
That's terrible! How can we help?

Eliza,
Why do people do that? I love animals!

Mike,
We need to change. I'll write my senator!

EnviroHelper,
Thank you for helping!

Chrystie,
No more poisons!

comments

"But it's not right," says Camila. "You're hurting other animals, too. All animals and plants are connected. They need each other. And we need them. There are other ways."

Camila's father looks at her. "Maybe. I'll think about it," he says.

Later, Camila and her mother visit Dr. Nez. The fox is better. "This fox was in trouble," says Dr. Nez. "Now it will live. You saved its life."

Camila feels happy. She takes a picture. She goes home. She posts it on the website.

Camila shows her father. "Look," she says. "We saved this fox. We can save more animals, too."

Her father smiles. "OK," he says. "I understand. We must help plants and animals. No more poison. We can find a new way."

cage

animal hospital

veterinarian

poison

medicine

herbivore

carnivore

pesticide